The Shepherd,

The Angel,

and Walter

The Christmas Miracle Dog

# THE SHEPHERD,

# THE ANGEL,

# AND WALTER

# THE CHRISTMAS

# MIRACLE DOG

# DAVE BARRY

Berkley Books
New York

THE BERKLEY PUBLISHING GROUP
Published by the Penguin Group
Penguin Group (USA) Inc.
375 Hudson Street, New York, New York 10014, USA
Penguin Group (Canada), 90 Eglinton Avenue East, Suite 700, Toronto, Ontario M4P 2Y3, Canada
(a division of Pearson Penguin Canada Inc.)
Penguin Books Ltd., 80 Strand, London WC2R 0RL, England
Penguin Group Ireland, 25 St. Stephen's Green, Dublin 2, Ireland (a division of Penguin Books Ltd.)
Penguin Group (Australia), 250 Camberwell Road, Camberwell, Victoria 3124, Australia
(a division of Pearson Australia Group Pty. Ltd.)
Penguin Books India Pvt. Ltd., 11 Community Centre, Panchsheel Park, New Delhi—110 017, India
Penguin Group (NZ), 67 Apollo Drive, Rosedale, North Shore 0745, Auckland, New Zealand
(a division of Pearson New Zealand Ltd.)
Penguin Books (South Africa) (Pty.) Ltd., 24 Sturdee Avenue, Rosebank, Johannesburg 2196,
South Africa

Penguin Books Ltd., Registered Offices: 80 Strand, London WC2R 0RL, England

PRINTING HISTORY
G. P. Putnam's Sons hardcover edition / November 2006
Berkley trade paperback edition / November 2008

Berkley trade paperback ISBN: 978-0-425-21774-0

The Library of Congress has cataloged the G. P. Putnam's Sons hardcover edition as follows:

Barry, Dave.
  The shepherd, the angel, and Walter the Christmas miracle dog/Dave Barry.
    p.   cm.
  ISBN 0-399-15413-2
  1. Christmas stories.   1. Title.
  PS3552.A74146S54   2006                         2006023183
  813'.54—dc22

PRINTED IN THE UNITED STATES OF AMERICA

10   9   8   7   6   5   4   3   2   1

*This book is dedicated to
the wonderful, quirky people
I grew up with in Armonk, New York.
Any resemblance between them
and the characters in this book is,
frankly, a bewildering coincidence.*

THE SHEPHERD,

THE ANGEL,

AND WALTER,

THE CHRISTMAS MIRACLE DOG

"*Luckies are easy on my throa*

There are no finer tobaccos than those used i
Luckies, and Luckies' exclusive process is you
throat protection against irritation...against coug

My name's Doug Barnes, and this stuff happened on Christmas Eve in my town, which is Asquont, New York. According to Mr. Purcell, who's my Social Studies teacher, Asquont is an Indian name that means some Indian thing like "Hunting Place in the Green Forest," but sometimes I think it was just a joke by the Indians to get white people to say "Asquont."

Anyway, there's no Indians here now, not in 1960. Also, this wouldn't be a good place to hunt anymore, unless you wanted to shoot somebody's station wagon. Asquont is only thirty miles from

New York City, which is where a lot of the dads work. In the morning they drive to North White Plains and take the train to New York, and at night they come home smelling like cigarettes. In between, they work and smoke.

My dad is one of them. He works for an advertising agency, which according to my mom means that he drinks martinis in the daytime. He does the commercials for Oldsmobile. We'll be watch-

ing TV, and when an Oldsmobile commercial comes on he'll go, "SHH!," and we all have to shut up and watch the commercial, like it was this great movie instead of a commercial with actors pretending to be a family, smiling like maniacs because they're so excited to be in their Oldsmobile.

My mom laughs at the commercials, especially the actress pretending to be the mother, who's wearing a dress and pearls and has her hair all fixed up. My mom says, "She looks just like me when I'm driving you kids to school in our lovely Oldsmobile station wagon, doesn't she, kids?" This cracks us up, because when Mom drives us to school she's usually wearing a bathrobe and hair curlers because she didn't have time to get dressed, because she had to get three of us kids ready for school and we're always late, mostly be-

cause of my little brother, Stuart, who is a total pain.

Like, one time we were getting into Mom's car, already late, and Stuart says, "Oh no! Today's the Science Fair!" And of course he forgot to do his Science Fair project, because that's the kind of total pain thing he does. So Mom said he'd just have to go to school without it, and Stuart started having a fit because he thought he was going to flunk, and finally Mom gave in, and they jumped out of the car and came up with a Science Fair project in, like, two minutes, which was pinecones. They ran around the yard picking up these pinecones and they put them in a shoe box, and that was going to be Stuart's Science Fair project. Don't ask me what scientific thing it was supposed to prove.

So by then we were really late, and Mom drove right to the front of the school, and just when we got there my little sister, Becky, who's not anywhere near as much of a pain as Stuart is but is real little, starts screaming: "THERE'S ANTS IN THE CAR, AND THEY'RE BITING ME." There were like ninety trillion red ants coming out of the pinecones and running around the backseat. So we all jumped out, and Mom was trying to brush the ants off the seat, and Becky and Stuart were crying because of ant bites, and I wanted to kill myself because just about every single kid in my school including Judy Flanders saw my mom in her bathrobe and curlers.

Judy Flanders is not my girlfriend, but I wish she was.

Anyway, now Mom's car has red ants in it and we can't get rid of them. Dad thinks they're living on food we dropped under the seat. They're pretty quiet when the car is cold, but once the heater warms it up you sometimes see them running around. Or we'll be driving somewhere and suddenly you'll feel something on your leg. Or sometimes you get bit. Like, one time we were going to church, and an ant bit Dad on the leg and he drove off the road and knocked over Mr.

Fabucci's mailbox. Dad said a really bad word, and me and Stuart laughed, and Mom told Dad he shouldn't use language like that in front of the kids, especially going to church, and Dad told Mom she should know better than to bring pinecones in a car, and Mom said, "Well, if you don't want pinecones in the car next time *you* can help the children with their Science Fair projects, *dear*," and they didn't talk at all the rest of the way to church.

Mom always says that being a housewife is a lot harder than being in advertising.

The church we go to is St. John's, which is Episcopal. It's on Route 218, in a row with the other two churches in Asquont, which are Methodist and Catholic. The Methodists don't set up a

Christmas manger scene outside in front of their church, but we do, and the Catholics do.

One Christmas a couple of years ago there was a Manger War. What happened was, early one Sunday morning somebody played a prank on the St. John's manger. When everybody got to church, Joseph and Mary were looking down at the baby Jesus like usual, but Joseph was wearing a New York Yankees hat, like he was this big Yankees fan. Some of the grown-ups were mad, but most of us kids thought it was pretty funny. The next day at school Tommy Mulroney, who's Catholic, was bragging that him and some other guys did it. So that night some of the older kids from our church went over to the Catholic church, St. Margaret's, and put a straw hat and a red bandanna on their Joseph, like he was Farmer Joseph. So the next night the Catholics put a hat and a tie and sunglasses on our Joseph, so he looked like this FBI agent investigating the baby Jesus. Also, they put a football helmet on one of our manger cows.

So far, everybody except the grown-ups thought it was pretty funny. But then the next night one of our guys, Warren Gartner, put his sister Elaine's bra on their Mary. That was a bad idea, because it turns out that Mary is a really big deal for the Catholics. The next day at school, Tommy Mulroney started shoving Warren in the cafeteria, and pretty soon everybody was shoving everybody, and there was this big fight between the Catholics and the Episcopalians, and also some

Methodist kids got involved. Guys were knocking each other down and throwing food, and Mrs. Forester, who's a science teacher and, like, 357 years old, got macaroni and cheese in her hair and went home early.

So the next day we had to go to this assembly where we got a lecture from Mr. Muller, the principal, who we call Mouse Muller because that's what he reminds everybody of, and Rev. Morrow, who was the priest at St. John's, and Father DiNardi, who was the priest at St. Margaret's, about how you should respect other people's religious beliefs. But it really wasn't about not respecting anybody's religion. It was really just kids hacking around. There wouldn't even have been a fight except that Warren Gartner had the idea about his sister's bra. She was so embarrassed she didn't come to school for, like, three days.

Pretty much all the girls in my class wear bras now. Kevin Smith, who sits at the back of my homeroom, keeps a list of who does and who doesn't. He started the list two years ago, when the first girl in our class got one. That was Donna "The Chest" West. She looks like she's at least eighteen or nineteen. She goes out with Joey Fragone, who is, like, thirty, because he got held back in school so many times. He smokes Lucky Strikes, and is the only kid in Asquont history that I know of who drove to junior high school.

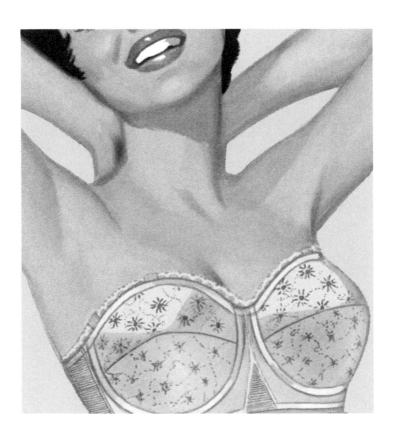

So after Donna came to school in a bra, Kevin started his list. When a girl came in with a bra for the first time, Kevin would go, "Janie Martin, you are ON THE LIST!" and the boys would all cheer. The girls hated this a lot, so of course Kevin kept doing it.

Last year maybe half the girls were on the list, but almost all the rest of them got on it at the beginning of this year. It was like they all went away to Summer Bosom Camp. When they came back, most of them looked a LOT older and taller than a lot of the boys. Me, for example. My mom says this is normal. "It all evens out in the end," she says. Which is easy for her to say because she's old and married, so it doesn't matter what she looks like. Meanwhile, I'm walking around like some kind of dwarf in the bosom forest.

I don't want it to all even out in the end. I want it to even out NOW. Because a lot of the girls in my class, now that they have bosoms and everything, are more interested in older boys, or at least cuter boys, which does not include me. Some of the girls hardly even talk to the boys in their own class anymore. They call us "children" if we're, like, making fart noises, which they used to think was funny.

One reason I like Judy Flanders, besides that she's kind of pretty and not too tall, is that she's nice, and she still talks to everybody, including me. She sits next to me in Science, and sometimes I can make her laugh. Like one time Mrs. Forester was doing a science demonstration that was pretty stupid involving freezing some water and then melting it again, and when she was finally done and the classroom was quiet I said, "So what you're saying, Mrs. Forester, is that ice is actually . . . frozen water!" Everybody cracked up except Mrs. Forester. Her face got real red, and she told me to go see Mr. Kinsella, who is the assistant principal. He gave me the same lecture he always gives me, about how I should stop wasting my brain being a clown, and then he thunked me on the head with the hand he wears his Iona College class ring on, which weighs, like, sixty-seven pounds. I think Mr. Kinsella kind of likes me, but he has to do his job.

Anyway, later that day I passed Judy Flanders in the hall, and she said it was pretty funny what I said to Mrs. Forester. I tried to think of something funny to say right then, but all I did was smile like a moron and make a sound like *Urg*. Later on, I thought of a whole bunch of funny things I could have said, but Judy Flanders didn't hear any of them. All she heard was *Urg*.

I think about Judy Flanders a lot, in case you didn't figure that out yet. Sometimes when I'm walking to school I imagine these conversations we could have, where I would make her laugh. One time, I went on an actual date with her, to the movies. I didn't ask her myself, though. What I did was, I told Phil Spenser that I wanted to go to the movies with Judy. Phil is my friend who really likes girls and is not afraid to talk to them. It's almost like a super power he has, like X-ray vision. He's sort of going steady with Sandy Schemmick, who is a friend of Judy's. So Phil told Sandy that I wanted to know if Judy wanted to go to the movies with me, and Sandy told Judy, and Judy told Sandy yes, and Sandy told Phil, who told me. I talked to Judy directly to figure out what day, but Phil was there just in case.

So one Saturday, Judy and I went to the movies in White Plains. Here's the thing, though: My mom drove. She tried not to embarrass me by talking or anything, but, still, there she was, in the front of the car. I sat in the back with Judy about two feet apart. We didn't talk much, either. Mostly I worried that she would get bit by a car ant and I would have to kill myself.

So it was pretty quiet all the way to White Plains. We went to the RKO Theater, and Judy and I sat near the front and my mom sat alone near the back. The movie was called *North to Alaska*, which had John Wayne and Fabian and punching. It was OK, I guess. I don't remember too much of it because of the situation with my right arm. When the movie started, I kind of perched my arm on the back of Judy's seat. My plan was to move it forward a little, so it was actually around Judy. I thought about this for a week ahead of time, having my arm around her. But I chickened out. I guess I was afraid that if my arm actually touched her, she'd go, Hey! What are you doing with your arm? And I would have to kill myself.

So for the whole movie, which seemed like seventy-nine hours long, I had my arm perched on the seat back, like, half an inch from Judy, and my arm fell asleep so bad that I didn't get the feeling all the way back until we were nearly in

Asquont again. When we got to Judy's house, I walked her to the door, but I didn't try to kiss her or anything because my mom was right there in the car, plus I didn't know if Judy would let me, plus I have never kissed anybody except practicing on the bathroom mirror.

The next Monday at school Judy told Sandy, and Sandy told Phil, and Phil told me, that Judy had a nice time on the date. I wanted to know a lot more stuff, like what would have happened if my arm touched her, and what about if I tried to kiss her, but Judy didn't say anything about that to Sandy, or if she did Sandy didn't tell Phil, so I still don't know.

That was my only date with Judy. Actually, it was my only date ever so far with anybody. But

sometimes I ask Judy to dance at Canteen. Canteen is this thing they have for Asquont kids on Friday night at Wayne C. Ferman Junior High School so we won't turn into juvenile delinquents. It costs fifty cents to get in. For the first hour, all the boys go into the gym and play basketball or just hack around, and all the girls go

into the cafeteria and fast-dance to records. Then the boys go into the cafeteria and mostly stand around watching the girls dance fast. Some boys dance fast, and the rest of us make fun of them. But I think the truth is, we wish we were dancing, too. I can do one fast dance, the Twist, which is pretty easy because you just rotate your feet back and forth. I learned it at home, in the bathroom looking in the mirror. But I'm too chicken to do it at Canteen.

At the end of the night, there's slow dancing. More of the boys dance then. I always try to dance with Judy Flanders. One time I danced with her to "Put Your Head on My Shoulder," and near the end she did kind of put her head on my shoulder. That was my best dance ever. But Judy is pretty popular, because she's nice and will dance with everybody, which some of the pretty girls won't. So usually there's a bunch of other guys who want to dance with her also and I don't always get a turn. There's one boy she dances with a lot, Kyle Decker. He moved to Asquont last year from California, and he's really good at sports. Which I'm not. He always asks Judy to dance at Canteen, and when they dance it makes me feel like somebody punched me in the stomach. I wish I knew if Judy likes him more than me, but there's no way to tell.

Everybody likes Kyle Decker. The teachers like him because he's smart and doesn't hack around in class. The girls like him because, according to them, he's cute. The boys like him because he's good at sports. I even kind of like him, except I hate that I think Judy likes him.

Anyway, Kyle and Judy both go to St. John's, and this year all three of us were in the Christmas pageant. The pageant is a really big deal at St. John's. On Christmas Eve, pretty much everybody goes to it, even the people who you never see at church. The pageant director is Mrs. Elkins, who's a tall, skinny lady with a lot of makeup whose hair is the exact same color as the orange part of a candy corn. She's been in charge of the pageant a LONG time. My dad says the first year she directed it, the part of the baby Jesus was played by the actual baby Jesus.

Mrs. Elkins used to be in The Theater in New York. She's really, really serious about the pageant. Like, if you're one of the Three Kings and the choir starts to sing "We Three Kings of

Orient Are," you better come out at the exact right time or Mrs. Elkins gets really hacked off.

I know this because last year I was a Three King. The other two were Phil Spenser and Mike Crane. During the pageant, we waited for our entrance in Rev. Morrow's office, which is right next to the sanctuary. We were supposed to come out bearing gifts of gold, frankincense and myrrh, which were played in the pageant by a vase and two wood boxes that Mrs. Elkins brought from her house. We were supposed to put these down next to the baby Jesus, which was played by a Betsy Wetsy doll, but from the audience you couldn't tell.

The Three Kings were supposed to come out as soon as we heard the organ start playing "We

Three Kings of Orient Are." But when the music started, Mike would sing, "We three kings of Orient are / Smoking on a rubber cigar." So we'd be laughing back there and we wouldn't come out on time, and Mrs. Elkins would get really mad.

She'd yell: "WHERE ARE MY KINGS? I WANT TO SEE KINGS AS SOON AS THE ORGAN STARTS!"

So we'd have to start over, but as soon as the organ started playing Mike would sing the cigar song again. You know how when you're not supposed to laugh, like at somebody's funeral, that's when you laugh the hardest and you can't stop, and it feels like you're going to pee your pants? That's what it was like. The three of us kings would sort of stagger out of Rev. Morrow's office making these squeaking noises from trying to hold the laughing in, like we were the Three Hamsters, and Mrs. Elkins would go: "WHAT IS SO FUNNY? DO YOU BOYS THINK THE BIRTH OF OUR LORD AND SAVIOR IS SOME SORT OF JOKE?" And she'd make us go back and do it *again*, and the next time Mike would only get part of the "we" out, so all he said was "wuh," and we were laughing so hard I had to hold on to Phil so I wouldn't fall over. So Mrs. Elkins stopped the rehearsal and gave us this huge lecture about how she was not volunteering her time as a person with years of experience as a Professional in The Theater so that we could turn a Sacred Religious Moment into some kind of juvenile Three Stooges comedy routine.

So anyway, on Christmas Eve the whole church was full for the pageant like it always is. We Three Kings were waiting back in Rev. Morrow's office wearing our costumes, which included crowns and itchy fake beards. When the organ started playing the Three Kings song, Phil and I thought for sure Mike was going to sing, so we were ready for that, and we were NOT going to laugh.

But Mike didn't sing. What he did, like, one second before we were supposed to go out was put an actual rubber cigar in his mouth, sticking out of his beard. Phil and I were cracking up so much

that Phil tripped on his robe and dropped Mrs. Elkins's vase, which broke in, like, a million pieces. By then, the choir was singing, and we had to go out, so Phil grabbed the Rolodex off of Rev. Morrow's desk. That's how the Three Kings went out, late, two of us squeaking like hamsters and one of us smoking a rubber cigar, bringing the baby Jesus gifts of gold, frankincense and a Rolodex. When Joseph, who was played by Jeffrey Reid, saw us, he started to crack up, and Wendy Hobart, who was Mary, pinched his arm really hard, so just when the narrator, who was played by Mr. Lundt because he has a deep voice, said the part about how the Wise Men worshipped the baby Jesus, Jeffrey went, "YEOW," and Phil tripped on his robe *again* and dropped the Rolodex on Betsy Wetsy Jesus, and Mike and I were laughing so hard that we had to run back into Rev. Morrow's office, and I actually did pee my pants a little bit.

A lot of kids told me after that it was a really great pageant, but Mrs. Elkins was pretty mad. She cornered Phil's, Mike's and my parents afterward, and went on and on about how she was volunteering her time and experience in The Theater and all she asked in return was a certain minimum amount of cooperation, and she had never in all her years in The Theater seen such disrespect, and she has as good a sense of humor as anyone but there is a limit, and if other people don't mind that their children are juvenile delinquents that is their business, but when it comes to making a mockery of the birth of Our Lord and Savior she has to speak out, not to mention the destruction of a vase that happened to be a souvenir of her trip to Mexico.

When Mrs. Elkins was finally done talking, my mom and dad walked toward me looking real serious. I thought I was going to get killed. But as soon as we got in the car, my dad busted out laughing. My mom was trying not to laugh, but then Dad said, "When you think about it, Jesus could *use* a Rolodex, to keep track of all the apostles," and Mom cracked up.

Then they got all serious and told me I was going to have to help pay for Mrs. Elkins's vase with my allowance. Then Mom said the pageant was about a sacred thing and it was nothing to joke about. Then it was real quiet in the car for a minute. Then Dad started humming "We Three

Kings of Orient Are" and Mom started laughing so hard that she fell over sideways in the front seat. Then Stuart got bit by an ant.

It was a really good Christmas.

This year, I was one of the shepherds in the pageant. It's better to be a shepherd than a Three King because, for one thing, you get to carry a stick. Also, instead of waiting in Rev. Morrow's office you wait at the back of the church, in the bell closet, where there's a steep little stairway that goes up to the attic, and a big rope that goes up to the bell in the steeple. The bell closet is way more interesting than Rev. Morrow's office, and kind of scary because of the bats.

There's like nineteen million bats living up in the St. John's attic. The thing about bats is, they poop. A lot. Nobody realized how much until what happened to Mr. Hemmitt a couple of years ago during the Easter service. Easter is a big deal at St. John's. It's like the second-biggest deal behind Christmas. Anyway, on Easter everybody in the whole congregation gets a potted hyacinth plant to take home. We have this tradition at St. John's, which I think is kind of goofy, where at the end of the service we sing a song that has a lot of "alleluias" in it, and on every alleluia we all raise our pots into the air, like we're offering our hyacinths to God or something. And at the end of the song, Mr. Hemmitt, who is this old guy in the church, goes into the bell closet and rings the bell a whole lot to celebrate because Jesus rose up from being dead.

So anyway, this one Easter a couple of years ago we were singing the alleluia song, and we got to the end and everybody was holding up their pots and kind of turning toward the bell closet waiting for the *bong*, so it was totally quiet in the church, and then instead of a *bong* there was a bad word and the closet door banged open and Mr. Hemmitt staggered out with this glop all over him, because when he started to pull the rope he brought this kind of bat-poop avalanche down on his head. A bunch of people ran over to him, and Mrs. Hemmitt screamed and dropped her pot. Mr. Hemmitt wasn't hurt bad or anything, but he didn't smell that great.

After that, the church formed a Bat Committee of men to try to do something. They hired a guy who went up into the attic and set off a smoke bomb to make the bats leave. Then he nailed up screening in the steeple so the bats couldn't get back in. Then Rev. Morrow did a blessing of the attic. And then, like, fifteen minutes later the bats came back. Dad says they must be Episcopalian bats.

The smoke-bomb guy told the Bat Committee there was a huge amount of bat poop in the attic that somebody should do something about. The committee decided it would have to get rid of the bats first. They tried a bunch of different things, but the bats always came back. Sometimes when you go into the bell closet, you can hear them rustling and flittering around up there in the dark. It's pretty cool.

The other two shepherds in the pageant this year were Mike and Phil. We were supposed to wait in the closet until the part of the Christmas pageant where the choir sings "While Shepherds Watched Their Flocks by Night." Then we were supposed to come out and have a little huddle in the church aisle, where we pretended we were deciding whether to go to Bethlehem, or what. Then we would walk to the front of the church where Joseph and Mary were waiting with the baby Jesus.

This year, Kyle Decker played Joseph. Mrs. Elkins picked him at the first rehearsal. She said he was a responsible young man with a head on his shoulders, unlike Some People she could name, meaning me and Phil and Mike. The thing is, usually I wouldn't want to be Joseph, because Joseph has to spend most of the pageant standing in the front of the church next to Mary, and Mary is usually some girl like Wendy Hobart who you wouldn't want to stand next to anyway.

But this year Mary was played by Judy Flanders. Which meant that for the rehearsals she was standing right next to Kyle. Sometimes I could see them whispering stuff to each other. Sometimes she would laugh at something he said, which was the worst. I tried to make her laugh, too, but it wasn't so easy since most of the time I was back in the bat closet with Mike and Phil.

At the first rehearsal, Mrs. Elkins gave us shepherds a big lecture about how she had not forgotten our behavior last year, and she certainly hoped there would be no incidents this year, because she would not want to have to call our parents, blah blah blah. I also got a lecture from my mom and dad, so I definitely didn't want to get in any trouble with Mrs. Elkins. Neither did Phil. But the thing about Mike is, he's one of those kids who if you tell him not to do anything he is pretty much going to do something. Phil and I knew he would, but we didn't know what it would be. We found out in the first rehearsal when we came out of the closet and we huddled to decide whether to go to Bethlehem. The three of us were in a little circle, looking at each other, and Mike said, "Shall we go to Bethlehem, men? Or shall we . . . *dance*?" Then, from under Mike's sweater, we heard Gary U.S. Bonds singing the song about New Orleans where he goes, "Hey, hey, hey, yeah." Not too loud, but you could hear it.

So of course Phil and I cracked up. Right away, Mrs. Elkins started stalking toward us like a really mad orange-haired stork, shouting: "WHAT IS GOING ON? WHAT ARE YOU SHEP-HERDS DOING?" By then, Mike had turned off his transistor radio, and he was looking inno-cent, like he didn't do anything, and all he wanted to do was get to Bethlehem already, and

Phil and I were holding him up. So Mrs. Elkins gave Phil and me the lecture about how she did not want to have to call our parents, blah blah blah.

Mike kept bringing the radio to rehearsals. We got better at not cracking up when we formed the shepherd huddle, but we never knew what song it would be, and sometimes Mike would turn it up pretty loud, so the church would be really quiet and suddenly, just for a second, you'd hear

"Teenager in Love," and Mrs. Elkins would dart her storky head around. She never figured out what was going on, but she was very suspicious. Of course the other kids in the pageant knew what was happening, and sometimes everybody would be laughing and Mrs. Elkins would have a fit. A couple of times, I saw Judy kind of laugh, but a couple of times I also saw her *not* laugh, so I couldn't tell if she thought it was funny or stupid. Mostly, I saw her talk to Kyle Decker. More and more I was wishing I could be Kyle Decker.

Anyway, we had five rehearsals. The last one was a dress rehearsal with the whole choir and the Host of Angels, which is a bunch of little kids, including this year my brother and sister, who are dressed as angels, and when they come out everybody goes, Awww. Mike almost made Phil and me laugh in the huddle when the radio played "Running Bear," but we held on and got through it without a lecture from Mrs. Elkins.

And then it was Christmas Eve.

I really like Christmas Eve. I think I like it even more than Christmas Day. On Christmas Day, you get to open your presents and see what you got, but you also know that Christmas is starting to be over for a year, and by nighttime some of the stuff you got is already broken. But on Christmas Eve, all the tree lights are on and carols are playing and people are saying "Merry Christmas," and everything is *about* to happen, but it didn't happen yet. That's the best time of the year.

But this year it didn't start out so great at our house, mostly because of our dog, Frank. He wasn't doing too good. The vet, Dr. Weingarten, said Frank wasn't sick so much as he was just getting too old. Frank was in our family a long time. Mom and Dad got him before they had me. He was a really big dog, much bigger than a regular dog. Dad always said he was a cross between a Labrador retriever and a Saint Bernard and an aircraft carrier. Frank scared some people, because when you came to our door he'd come charging at you, barking so loud it could hurt your ears. But it was a happy bark, and it just meant that Frank wanted to meet you and lick you. He was a big licker. Dad always said that if robbers ever came to our house, Frank would lick them into submission.

Frank also liked to sort of swallow people's hands, not to eat them or anything but to see what the people tasted like. You'd be watching TV or something and suddenly your hand would feel warm and wet, and you'd look down to see it was pretty far into Frank's mouth, and he'd be looking at you with this happy look, like he was saying, "Wow! You taste great!" We were used to this, but it sometimes took guests by surprise, like the Thanksgiving when Frank tasted Aunt Nancy's hand from behind and she screamed and threw her punch glass across the living room.

Frank was the kind of dog who pretty much loved everybody except squirrels. Whenever you walked into a room where he was lying, he'd jump up and give you a big Frank-style greeting, licking you and tasting your hand and wagging his whole rear end to let you know how good you tasted. If you left the room, even for only thirty seconds, when you got back Frank would jump up and get excited all over again, like he hadn't seen you for five years. He did that for everybody. But his absolute favorite person in the world was my sister, Becky. The day she came home from the hospital, he slept in her room, and that's where he slept from then on. Before Becky could walk, she would get around by grabbing on to Frank's fur and kind of hauling herself up next to him, and the two of them would go around that way, Becky hanging on to Frank, taking little

wobbly steps, and Frank grinning his big old Frank grin.

When Becky said her first word, it was "Fank." Mom said, "Well, I guess I know where I stand."

When Mom would take Becky for a walk in her stroller, Frank would be right next to them, and if another dog came near — even a dog that Frank was friends with — Frank would make a real low growl and the other dog would go away. When Becky got older and would be out playing in the neighborhood, Frank was right there watching her. Mom always said she never had to worry because Becky had the world's best nanny.

Besides being with Becky, Frank's favorite thing in the world was riding in the car. Whenever it looked like anybody might be going out, Frank would charge to the front door. Sometimes he would run headfirst right into the door because he was so excited that he might be going on a car trip. There'd be this *bang* when his head hit the door and he'd bounce back a few feet, then look at the door, like, Whoa! Who put THAT there? If Frank was outside and the car windows were down, he'd jump into the car and wait, in case the car might go somewhere. He always sat in the driver's seat, like he thought maybe this time he was going to drive. But when he actually did go somewhere, he would sit in the back with his head stuck out the window so he could bark at squirrels.

That was his enemy, the squirrels. Frank hated them. It was like he thought they were all of a sudden going to stop running around with acorns and attack the Oldsmobile. We all thought it was pretty funny until Frank's accident. That was two years ago. We were driving on Route 218 when Frank saw a squirrel, and he must have thought it was a really dangerous-looking squirrel because he jumped out the car window to get it.

The thing was, we were going, like, fifty miles an hour. Becky screamed, and Dad stopped the car and we all ran back, and Frank was lying by the side of the road, and right away you could see something was wrong with his legs. He was hurt bad, but when Becky got to him he kind of thumped his tail on the ground to let her know he was sorry he couldn't get up and say hi but he was glad to see her.

So now Becky was screaming and Stuart was crying and Mom was crying and I was probably crying a little bit. Dad and I picked Frank up, which was hard because Frank was heavy, and he made this awful crying sound when we moved him. We took him home and put him on a blanket in the garage, and Becky sat down next to him and would not move. Mom called Dr. Weingarten, and he came over and looked at Frank. Then he talked quietly to Mom and Dad. I went over by them and heard Dr. Weingarten say they might have to put Frank to sleep, but Mom and Dad looked at Becky, who was sitting on the blanket petting Frank, who was thumping his tail a little, and they said absolutely not. So Dr. Weingarten put casts on three of Frank's legs and gave him some shots and a lot of medicine, and said let's hope for the best.

For the next three nights, Becky slept on the blanket next to Frank and hardly left the garage except to go to the bathroom. For a while Frank seemed to be getting worse. He wouldn't eat at all, and he barely opened his eyes. Once, I heard Mom and Dad talking in the kitchen about what Dr. Weingarten said about putting him to sleep. Then Mom looked at Becky in there on the blanket with Frank and cried.

On the third day Frank wasn't moving at all, and you could barely tell he was breathing. I think Mom and Dad were about to call Dr. Weingarten to come put him to sleep. That was when Becky came into the kitchen and said, "Frank needs a squirrel."

Dad and Mom told her that Frank was very sick

and a squirrel wouldn't help him, besides which we didn't have any squirrels. But Becky was sure a squirrel would perk Frank up. She started crying really hard, and Mom and Dad were trying to talk to her but she wouldn't listen. She was just sobbing and sobbing, and everybody felt horrible.

Mom and Dad and I were standing around trying to figure out how to make Becky stop crying when Stuart came downstairs and asked what was wrong. I told him, and he said, "I know where there's a squirrel."

Stuart is usually a total pain who never has any good ideas, but it turned out he really did know where a squirrel was. It was on the side of the road, and it was dead, but that's probably the only kind of squirrel we could have caught. Stuart and I put it in a shoe box and brought it home and gave it to Becky. She took the shoe box and punched some holes in the side with a pencil so the smell could get out. Then she took it into the garage and set it down next to Frank's nose and said, "Here, Frank, I brought you a squirrel."

Mom and Dad and Stuart and I were watching from the kitchen doorway. For a minute, Frank didn't do anything. But then, without opening his eyes, he thumped his tail two times, like he was saying thank you. Becky looked at us and said, "See? He feels better."

And she was right, because that night Frank started getting better. The next day he ate some food, and a few days later he could sort of stand up. Dr. Weingarten said Becky had discovered a new treatment: the Squirrel Cure. In a couple of months Frank was sort of his old self again, except that he ran slower, and sometimes needed help to get into the car. But he stayed in a good mood, even when he started to not be able to see and hear so well, so that when somebody came to the door Becky would have to go, "Frank! Somebody's at the door!" so he would know to bark and go to the door and taste whoever it was.

Then this year around Thanksgiving, Frank started acting pretty sick. Dr. Weingarten said it wasn't anything he could give medicine for. He said, "Frank is just wearing out."

After Thanksgiving, Frank got worse. He could barely get up the stairs to Becky's room at night.

Mom and Dad started talking to Becky about it, telling her that one day Frank might leave us. Becky's six but she's not stupid, so right away she knew when they said leave us they meant die. She wanted to know what happened to dogs after they died, and Mom said they go to heaven. So Becky asked who took care of dogs in heaven, and Mom said Jesus did. So Becky asked if there were squirrels in heaven, and Mom said she was sure there were.

The week before Christmas, Frank got even worse, and on Christmas Eve nobody in our house felt very Christmasy. Especially not Dad. He was down in the basement, trying to put together Stuart's present, which was supposed to be a bicycle. Dad isn't so good at being handy with tools. Like one time, he tried to make us a tree house from this article he saw in *Popular Mechanics*. The picture in the article looked like you would end up with this actual little house up in a tree, but the one Dad made looked more like a giant insect. Right away boards started falling off, and after a couple of days most of the tree house was on the lawn. Sometimes we tease Dad about building us another lawn house, which he doesn't think is funny.

Anyway, on Christmas Eve, Dad was working on Stuart's bicycle, which was supposed to be a surprise from Santa Claus. We heard Dad clanking around in the basement and sometimes shouting bad words. Finally, Mom told me to go tell Dad that pretty soon we needed to get ready for the Christmas pageant. So I went downstairs, and there was Dad, sitting on the floor in the middle of like sixteen thousand bicycle pieces. It didn't look like they were going to form into a bicycle anytime soon. Dad was looking at a big piece of paper covered with instructions. He asked me if I knew what a *grommet* was. I said I never heard of it. He said he never heard of it, either. He told me to promise that if I ever had children, I would never buy them anything that required assembly. So I promised, then told him that Mom said we

had to get ready to go to the pageant. He said to tell Mom he would be up just as soon as he found his Phillips screwdriver so he could commit suicide with it.

When I went back upstairs, Mom was standing by the kitchen door, and she looked upset. She looked around to make sure Becky wouldn't hear, then she told me she was worried about Frank, because he'd been outside for a long time and he didn't come when she called him for dinner, which was not normal. She asked me to go outside and look for him. So I got my coat and went out.

It was really cold, the way it gets in winter when there's no clouds. Even though it was nighttime, I could see pretty far because the ground was covered with snow and there were like a billion stars out.

I saw Frank right away. He was standing over by the tree where Dad tried to make the tree house. I called him but he didn't move. I walked toward him and called a couple more times, but he still didn't move. I started to have a bad feeling.

When I got to Frank, I saw he was kind of leaning against the tree. I put my hand on his back and said his name. His fur was still soft, but underneath he felt hard, and he didn't move at all. I said his name again, but by then I knew. I ran back to the kitchen, and as soon as Mom saw me she said, "Oh no." I tried to say something to her but my throat wouldn't work. So she gave

me a hug, then got her coat and went outside for a while. When she came back, her eyes were all red.

She went into the TV room and told Becky and Stuart to go upstairs and get ready for the pageant. Then she yelled down to the basement for Dad. When he came upstairs and saw Mom's face, he said what is it and Mom said, "Frank." Dad didn't say anything, he just hugged Mom for a long time. Then he asked where Frank was and Mom said out back by the oak, and Dad said he would move him before Becky saw him. And Mom said, "How are we going to tell her?" Dad said he didn't know how, but they'd have to tell her by bedtime, because she'd know something was wrong when Frank didn't come to her room.

And Mom said, "This is going to ruin her Christmas."

Then they talked about what to do with Frank. They thought about burying him, but Dad said the ground was frozen solid. So they decided that Dad and I would put Frank into the station wagon and take him to the animal shelter in Pennsbridge, then go to the pageant. Mom would take Stuart and Becky in Dad's car and meet us at church.

So Mom dried her face and went upstairs to get Stuart and Becky ready, and I went back out with Dad to where Frank was standing. For a little while, Dad just looked at him. Then he patted him one time on the head and said, "Good dog."

Then he said it again, "Good dog," but he couldn't get the words all the way out.

After a little while more of standing there, Dad said, "OK." We each took an end of Frank and picked him up. He was heavy but he was really stiff, so it wasn't too bad carrying him. We put him in the back of the station wagon and laid him down sideways, like he was sleeping. Dad patted him on the head again and said, "Good dog." Then we went back inside.

Mom had Stuart and Becky in their pageant costumes. They were both in the Host of Angels, so they had robes on and halos on their heads, and they were holding wings to put on later. Becky asked where Frank was because she wanted to hug him good-bye. Mom and Dad looked at each other, and Dad said Frank was outside, and before Becky could say anything else Mom said, "Come on, kids, we don't want to be late for the pageant," and she bustled Becky and Stuart into their coats and out to Dad's car.

I went upstairs and put on my shepherd's costume, then Dad and I got into the station wagon and drove to Pennsbridge. It felt weird being in the car with Frank in the back. We didn't say anything, except for one time when Dad said he hoped the animal shelter was still open. Dad turned on the radio and it was playing "It Came Upon a Midnight Clear."

When we got to the animal shelter, it looked closed. We got out and Dad knocked on the door, but nobody came, and Dad said a bad word. He knocked a couple more times, and we were about to leave when the door unlocked and an old guy opened it. He said they were closed, but Dad said it was an emergency because we had to drop off a dog. The old guy said, "On Christmas Eve?" And Dad said yes. So the old guy said, "OK, let's have a look." He came outside, and Dad opened the tailgate and showed him Frank. The old guy leaned in and looked at Frank for a minute, then touched him. Then he ducked back out and said, "Sir, this dog is dead."

And Dad said, "I know."

And the old guy said, "We don't take dead animals at the animal shelter. We only take live animals."

And Dad said, "But it's Christmas Eve."

And the old guy said, "Sir, even on Christmas Eve we don't take dead animals."

So Dad asked the old guy if anybody around Pennsbridge did take dead animals, and the old guy said not on Christmas Eve. He said sorry, and Merry Christmas anyway. And Dad said, "Yeah."

So the guy went back to the shelter, and I got back into the car because it was really cold. Dad opened the car door on his side and stood there for a second, trying to think what to do with Frank. He was standing like that when the old guy started to open the shelter door and yelled, "Hey!"

He yelled that because as soon as he had the door open a crack, a huge dog came busting out. It ran right past the old guy and right past Dad, and it jumped into the car and sat in the driver's seat next to me. He leaned over and gave me a quick lick. Then he looked out the windshield and made a happy little bark, like he was saying: I'm ready! Let's go!

The old guy came running back to our car going, "Walter! Get out of there!" He grabbed hold of the dog's collar and pulled, but this was a really big dog and it seemed to want to stay in the car. Dad said, "I'll give you a hand," and he reached in and the dog opened his mouth and tasted Dad's hand practically up to his elbow. And Dad said, "Well, he's friendly." And the old guy said, "He certainly seems to like you."

Dad asked why the dog was in the shelter. The

old guy said he was with an elderly couple who really loved him but he was a little too rambunctious for them, and sometimes he ran off after squirrels. The old guy said he was a nice dog, but sometimes it was harder to place a big, rambunctious dog. Dad said, "What happens if you can't place him?" The man said eventually they would have to put him to sleep. He said they hated to do it but they had no choice because there were animals coming in all the time.

Now Dad was squatting next to the car, looking at the dog. He said, "His name is Walter?" And the old guy said, "Yes, Walter, and he has all his shots."

I said, "He looks a lot like Frank, except lighter brown."

Dad said, "I was thinking the same thing."

Then we looked at each other.

Then Dad said to the old guy, "Is it too late to adopt a dog tonight?" And the old guy said it was, but he would make an exception since it was Christmas Eve, and he would even give us the special shepherd discount.

A half hour later, the four of us—Dad, me, Frank and Walter—were driving back to Asquont. Dad was getting nervous. One reason was, it was almost time for the pageant to start and I was supposed to be at the church already. Another reason was, Dad was worried that maybe Walter was not such a great idea because Becky might not be ready for a new dog so soon after Frank was gone. Also we still had Frank in the car and Dad needed to do something with him and he still didn't have any ideas for that, and neither did I.

About three miles from Asquont, the car suddenly started bumping and going *blut-blut-blut-blut*, which meant we had a flat. Dad said a bad word and steered to the side of the road. We got out of the car and so did Walter. Dad opened the tailgate to get out the jack, which was next to Frank. Walter came over and gave Frank a sniff. Dad got out the tire-changing stuff and started trying to change the tire and right away he had trouble, which was not unusual because there were tools involved.

I knew Dad wasn't going to get the tire fixed anytime soon. Definitely not in time to take me to the pageant. Plus, I was freezing, because all I had under my coat was my shepherd costume, which is pretty much a bathrobe. So I asked Dad if I could walk to St. John's. He said he didn't want me on the road at night, but I said I wouldn't go on the road because we were next to the hill that goes up to the Palmers' orchard and if you just go up there there's a path down the other side that comes out almost right at the church. I told Dad I've taken that path, like, a million times, which was not exactly true, but I did take it once. Also I told Dad I was freezing, and Mrs. Elkins would have a fit if I missed the pageant.

Finally, Dad said OK. He said to tell Mom what happened, and he would get to the church as soon as he got the tire fixed and dropped Walter off at home. I asked him what he was going to do with Frank and he said he would figure something out.

So I got my shepherd stick and started up the hill. For a little while I could hear Dad saying bad words, but then he faded away and it got really quiet, except for my feet crunching in the snow. When I got to the top of the hill, I stopped for a minute and caught my breath and looked at the stars. I don't think I ever saw that many stars in the sky before.

I started to walk through the orchard, which felt a little weird because the trees were all bare and made a lot of kind of strange shapes. I was thinking I would be really glad to get through the orchard.

Then I thought I heard a noise. I turned around, but I didn't see anything. I started walking a little faster, kind of almost running. Then my heart completely stopped beating because I heard something running behind me, crunching the snow. I grabbed my shepherd stick with both hands and turned around real fast.

Next thing I knew I was lying on my back in the snow with Walter standing on me. He was licking my face to let me know he was happy to see me. I was also pretty happy to see him, except for the part about lying in the snow.

Finally, I got him off me and stood up. I figured he ran away from Dad and followed me, but I wasn't sure what to do about it. First I thought I should take Walter back to Dad. But if I did that,

I'd miss the pageant for sure. Plus, I thought maybe Dad would have the tire fixed and he might be driving along the road looking for Walter. Plus, I really wanted to get someplace warm. I couldn't feel my ears anymore. All I had on my head was my shepherd head thing, which I guess is fine in a desert but no good in an orchard when it's, like, zero degrees.

So I decided I would take Walter with me to the church. My plan was to put him in the basement, where we have Sunday school, until the pageant was over. I told Walter, "Here, boy," and I started to walk again. Walter stayed right with me, which made me feel better because the orchard was definitely feeling spooky. Also it was feeling bigger than I remembered. Either that or I wasn't going in a straight line, because I kept walking and

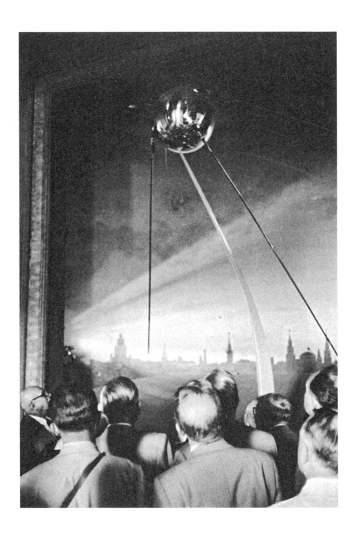

walking and I still wasn't out of it. I started to feel
definitely lost.

Finally, I stopped. Walter stopped, too. He sat
down in the snow and kind of leaned up against
me, which made me feel a little better because it
was exactly what Frank used to do. I said to myself, OK, try to figure this out. I turned all the
way around really slow. Every direction looked
like the same thing: spooky trees. Then I looked
up at the sky. If you know where the North Star
is, you can figure out which way north is. But I
didn't know which one was the North Star, and,
even if I did, I didn't know whether I needed to
go north, or what.

Anyway, while I was looking up with Walter
leaning against me I saw this one star that looked

brighter than the other ones. At first I thought it might be the North Star, but then I realized it was moving. Not fast but definitely moving. Which meant it wasn't a star; it was a satellite. I didn't know which one it was. The Russians sent up the first one, *Sputnik*, when I was in fifth grade. It was a big deal, and everybody got real upset because the Russians beat us into space. The teachers said we had to work harder in math and science. They made it sound like it was our fault, like the Russians built their satellite first because the fifth graders at Asquont Elementary weren't learning decimals fast enough.

Anyway, America finally started catching up, and now there's a bunch of satellites up there. A few times my family went out on the lawn and looked for them, but we never saw one, although Stuart claimed he did, but he didn't. But this was definitely a satellite. It was really bright, and it was going right over my head.

So I decided to follow it. I know that sounds weird, following a satellite, but I was really cold and really lost, and I needed to go in some direction, and I picked that one. So I patted Walter on the head and said, "Come on, boy," and we started walking.

You probably won't believe this, but it's true: The satellite led us straight to the path. I think it must have been an American satellite. In, like, ten minutes Walter and I were walking down the other side of the hill, and I could see the sign for the Asquont Pharmacy, and then the St. John's steeple.

When we got near the church I could hear people singing "O Come, All Ye Faithful," so I knew the service was already going, and they were getting close to the shepherd part. The parking lot was full. I didn't see our station wagon. I went around the side of the church, where you go downstairs to the basement, so I could put Walter in there.

But the door was locked.

By then I was so cold I was shivering all the time, just one big, long shiver. Plus, I had to be in the pageant. So I had to go inside. But I couldn't leave Walter alone outside. So I decided to take him into the main part of the church. There's two main doors, and the one on the right-hand side is right next to the bell-rope closet at the back of the church, where the shepherds wait. I figured I could take Walter in that way real quick, and he could stay in the closet while I went out with Mike and Phil to be shepherds, and then I could get him after the pageant.

It almost worked out pretty good.

When I opened the door to go into the church, everybody was standing up and singing "Angels We Have Heard on High," with the parts where everybody goes *Glooo-ooo-ooo-ri-a*. It was pretty loud, and everybody was looking toward the front of the church, so nobody saw me and Walter come in. I had Walter by the collar and pulled him really quick over to the bell closet and opened the door and pulled him inside and closed the door.

Mike and Phil were in there, wearing their shepherd costumes. Walter gave them both a lick of hello, and Phil said, "You brought your DOG? To the PAGEANT?" And Mike said, "Cool." So I tried to explain about the flat tire and everything, but then the song ended and Phil said, "Shhh." We could hear Mr. Lundt, the narrator, starting the part about how there were shepherds abiding in the fields keeping watch over their flocks by night, which meant it was time for Mike and Phil and me to go out and decide whether to go to Bethlehem.

So I said to Walter, "Stay!" Walter gave me a big smile and wagged his tail like he totally understood. Then he ran up the stairs to the attic. It's a narrow stairway, and Walter's a big dog, but he was gone in a second. He must have smelled the bat smell up there. I started to go up after him, but Phil grabbed me and said, "We have to go out — NOW!" He was right, because we could hear Mr. Lundt, sounding a little annoyed, repeating the part about how there were shepherds abiding in the fields keeping watch over their flocks by night.

So Phil opened the closet door, and the three of us went out and started walking up the aisle with our shepherd sticks. Everybody in the whole congregation was turned around to look at us. Way up in the front, in the middle, I could see Judy Flanders standing next to Kyle Decker by the cradle with the baby Jesus Betsy Wetsy doll. Judy had her Mary costume on and looked really pretty. Kyle Decker looked like he always looks, which is perfect. On the left was the Heavenly

Host of Angels, including Stuart and Becky. Off to the side on the right was Mrs. Elkins, who was holding a clipboard and giving us a glare for being late coming out of the closet.

When Mr. Lundt saw us come out he start reading the part about how an angel of the Lord came upon the shepherds and told them fear not because there were good tidings about a savior, which would be a babe in swaddling clothes laying in a manger. This was the part where we were supposed to form a huddle and decide to go to Bethlehem, and then the choir would sing "Silent Night."

That was what was supposed to happen. Here's what happened.

First, when we got into the huddle, with the whole church watching, Mike whispered, "Shall we go to Bethlehem, men? Or shall we ... *dance*?" And he reached under his shepherd bathrobe, and Phil and I are looking at him like, you're not going to do that in the actual PAGEANT. But this was Mike, so of course he was. I don't think he meant it to come out as loud as it did. I think he just wanted us to hear it so we would crack up. But he turned it up too far, and all of a sudden, in this totally quiet church with everybody looking at the shepherds, out of the huddle comes Brenda Lee singing "Rockin' Around the Christmas Tree." And Mike got this look on his face like Yikes and tried to turn it off, but he was fumbling around with the radio and he just made it louder.

The second thing that happened was that Mrs. Elkins came storking down the aisle toward us. From the way she was looking at us, I'm pretty sure she would have tried to kill us with her clipboard. But we never found out because of the third thing that happened.

That was a noise. It was a really loud, long noise of something cracking, like *craaaaaaaaaack*, and it was coming from the front of the church. Everybody turned around to look. At first nobody saw what was happening, but then somebody yelled, "The ceiling!" And everybody looked up, and people started screaming. Because right over where Judy and Kyle were standing with the baby Jesus, the ceiling was getting this giant bulge, and pieces of plaster were falling.

Kyle looked up and saw that the ceiling was coming down, and right away he took off running. But not Judy. A piece of plaster landed on her head and broke into a dust cloud, and she was holding her head and looking kind of confused. I don't think she knew the ceiling was coming down. So I dropped my shepherd stick and started running toward her. I was yelling for her to move out of the way, but by then a lot of people were screaming and yelling so she didn't hear me, and when I got to the front of the church the ceiling bulge was bulging way down so I just kept right on running toward her, and just when I got there I heard this really loud sound right over us and I kind of dove at Judy and pushed her as hard as I could back toward the altar in a kind of tackle, and then there was this giant *WHAM*, and it sounded like the whole church fell down behind us.

I didn't see what happened because I was lying on top of Judy on the floor and there was plaster and some boards on top of us and there was dust everywhere. But later on people told me what happened.

Right when I tackled Judy, this giant piece of ceiling came crashing down. But it wasn't just ceiling. On top of the ceiling was a chunk of frozen bat poop that was like the size of a car. Later on, they figured out that it weighed more than a ton. The bats took years to make it. It was sitting up there all that time, pressing on the ceiling, waiting to come down.

The reason it came down right then was Walter. Dad said he was the straw that broke the bat poop's back. When the ceiling came down, Walter was standing on top of this giant frozen chunk, like it was his magic carpet, except it was going straight down. When it hit the floor, it went *WHAM* and broke into pieces, and Walter hopped off, looking a little surprised to suddenly be in the church, but also happy to be there.

He ran straight to Becky.

Mom saw it because she was trying to get to Becky and Stuart, who were up with the rest of the Heavenly Host, right next to where the ceiling fell. Mom was having trouble getting there because she was stuck in the middle of a pew, and everybody was yelling and trying to get out at

once. But she saw Walter run straight to Becky, who was kind of crouched on the floor looking really scared. Walter gave her a giant lick, and she looked at him, and he gave her another giant lick, and she put her arms around his neck and hugged him tight, and the two of them just stayed that way until Mom got there.

Like I said, I didn't see this because I was lying on top of Judy Flanders with a bunch of junk on us. Right away, Rev. Morrow and some other men were around us getting stuff off us and asking if we were OK, which we both were, but they made us sit there for a few minutes while they got Dr. Monte to come look at us. While we were sitting there, looking at the big mess of stuff that almost landed on us, Judy said to me, "I think maybe you saved my life." I don't remember what

I said back. I think it was something like *Urg*. But I felt really great.

Pretty soon, a bunch of people were cleaning up the ceiling mess, but nobody was leaving the church. In fact, more people were showing up. Dad was one of them. He finally got the tire changed, but only because Mr. Liuzzo, who owns the Esso station, stopped and helped him. Also the entire Asquont Volunteer Fire Department came. It wasn't really a fire kind of emergency, but when people heard that the St. John's ceiling collapsed during the Christmas pageant because of a giant thing of frozen bat poop, everybody wanted to see it. Also a lot of people from the Methodists and the Catholics came over when their Christmas Eve services ended to find out what all the commotion was at St. John's.

It took a while for everybody to figure out what happened. Especially people wanted to know how a dog nobody ever saw before ended up in the church ceiling. So Dad explained how we got Walter at the animal shelter, although he left out the part about Frank since Becky was listening. Then I explained how Walter got up in the ceiling. I said I felt kind of bad about that because that's why the ceiling collapsed. But Rev. Morrow said yes, but it was going to collapse anyway, sooner or later, and it could have been a lot worse. He said it was a miracle nobody was hurt, even Walter, who Rev. Morrow said was a "miracle dog." Everybody laughed and looked at Walter, who was still standing right next to Becky, who still had her arms around him. Just then, Mrs. McCaffrey, who was helping with the cleanup, found the Betsy Wetsy

Jesus doll under a board and there was not a
scratch on it, and everybody said that was incred-
ible.

So by then there were still all these people there
from three different churches. And Rev. Morrow
said we never got to finish our pageant. He asked
where Mrs. Elkins was, and somebody said that
when the ceiling collapsed Mrs. Elkins set her
clipboard down on a pew, then turned around
and walked out of the church without even putting her coat on. So Rev. Morrow said maybe this
would be a good time for a prayer. So we all
bowed our heads, and Rev. Morrow said a prayer
about how maybe we were all from different
churches but we all worship the same God, and
sometimes He works in mysterious ways, and He
definitely worked in a mysterious way this time

to bring us all together on Christmas Eve. And even though it was a prayer, everybody kind of laughed, but it was OK.

Then Mrs. Morrow, who leads the choir, started to sing "Joy to the World," and everybody joined in, and it sounded really good, all those people singing at once.

By then it was pretty late and people started to leave. Before she left with her mom and dad, Judy Flanders came over to me and said thank you again, and see you in school, and Merry Christmas. I said you're welcome, and OK, and Merry Christmas. Then she smiled at me and left with her parents. Even with plaster in her hair, she's beautiful.

My family was one of the last ones to leave the church. Dad said he needed to talk to Mom for a minute, so I should wait with Stuart and Becky and Walter. Mom and Dad went a little way away, and Dad was saying something. I heard him say the name Walter a couple of times. Mom was pretty upset. She kept looking over at Becky with a real worried look. I heard Dad say don't worry, it'll be OK, but I could tell Mom wasn't sure.

So finally they came back, and we walked out of the church, and it was snowing. It was like a perfect Christmas Eve snow, with the big, fluffy kind of snowflakes that turn everything white real fast. We just stood and looked at it for a minute. Then Dad said why don't we all ride home together, we can get my car tomorrow, and Mom said OK, because she doesn't like driving in the snow anyway. So Dad started walking toward the station wagon. I said, "Dad," and gave him a look to remind him about Frank being in the back of the station wagon. He just nodded and didn't say anything.

We got to the station wagon and started brushing the snow off it, and right away I saw that Frank wasn't in the back anymore. We got in the car, with Dad and Mom and me in the front, and Becky and Stuart and Walter in the back. Dad started the motor, and we started driving out of the parking lot onto Route 218.

And Becky said, "We're going to keep Walter, right?"

And Mom and Dad both said, "Yes, of course we are."

Then Mom turned around and looked at Becky really serious, and said, "Honey, I have to tell you something."

And Becky said, "What?"

And Mom said, "Honey, Frank is gone."

And Becky said, "I know."

Dad stopped the car. He and Mom both said, "You do?"

And Becky said, "Frank is with Jesus."

Now we were all looking at Becky. And Becky was looking out the window. She pointed, and said, "There he is."

So we all looked. She was pointing at the St. John's manger scene. There were Joseph and Mary, looking down at the Baby Jesus. Next to them, also looking at Jesus, were two sheep and two cows. And next to one of the cows, kind of leaning against it, also looking at Jesus, was Frank.

Mom gave Dad a look, like, Are you CRAZY? And he leaned over across me and whispered to Mom that he couldn't think of anyplace else to put Frank, and would come back and get him first thing tomorrow.

And Becky said, "When will Jesus and Frank go to heaven?"

And Mom said, "Very soon, honey."

And Becky said, "Will the cows go, too?"

And Mom said yes.

And Becky said good. She was quiet for a second, and Dad started to move the car again. And then Becky waved, and said, "Good-bye, Frank."

And then we all said good-bye to Frank.

And then we drove away.

So that was Christmas Eve.

On Christmas Day, Dad was pretty tired because he was up late swearing at Stuart's bicycle, plus he went out real early. When he came back, he told me and Mom that he took Frank to the Petersons, who said they'd keep him in their shed until we could bury him. Then we got Becky and Stuart and opened the presents.

Becky got a Barbie doll, which was what she wanted. Stuart got his bike, only he couldn't ride it because of the snow, plus it only had one pedal, and the handlebars were backward. Dad promised he would fix it, which made Stuart cry, so Mom promised that she would take the bike to Liuzzo's garage the next day and have Mr. Liuzzo fix it and then Stuart was OK. I got a vibrating football game where you line up the players, then turn on a motor and the vibrating makes the players move. Usually they go in the completely wrong direction, or turn around in circles or just fall down, but it's fun anyway. I gave Dad a belt and Mom a perfume from the drugstore. They acted surprised, even though that's what I always get them.

Nobody got Walter anything because we didn't know we'd have him, but he didn't care. We took him out in the snow and he ran around at, like, four hundred miles an hour knocking everybody over and then licking them, which was exactly what Frank used to do.

I'm not saying we felt like Walter replaced Frank, because Frank was Frank and you couldn't replace him. It was more like Walter was reminding us what was so great about Frank, which was that no matter what kind of mood everybody else was in, he was always in a good one. For Frank, it was always Christmas Day, and you could tell Walter felt the same way.

The only bad part of that Christmas Day was when Mom and Dad told me I had to call up

Mrs. Elkins and apologize. When I dialed the phone, I had this bad feeling in my stomach because I thought she'd be really mad at me. But you know what? She wasn't. In fact, she was in this weirdly good mood. She seemed like she really wanted to talk to me, like I was a grown-up instead of a kid who wrecked her pageant. She told me that when she left the church she drove home and had a good cry and a glass of sherry, and then another one. She said by the third glass of sherry, she realized that she needed to stop acting like she was on Broadway because she wasn't on Broadway, she was directing the St. John's Christmas pageant, and the whole point of Christmas is to love your fellow man, even if your fellow man brings a large dog AND a radio to your pageant. And I said the radio wasn't me. And she said, "Oh, I know, it was that Michael

Crane boy who brought the radio, and you tell
him that if he does that again next year I'll wring
his neck." But she was laughing when she said it.

Finally Mrs. Elkins wound down, and she said,
"Merry Christmas, Douglas." I said Merry